FOODS OF INDIA

by Christine Velure Roholt

BELLWETHER MEDIA • MINNEAPOLIS, MN

Library of Congress Cataloging-in-Publication Data

VeLure Roholt, Christine, author.
 Foods of India / by Christine VeLure Roholt.
    pages cm. -- (Express. Cook with Me)
 Summary: "Information accompanies step-by-step instructions on how to cook Indian food. The text level and subject matter are intended for students in grades 3 through 7"-- Provided by publisher.
 Audience: Age 7-12.
 Audience: Grades 3-7.
 Includes bibliographical references and index.
 ISBN 978-1-62617-118-3 (hardcover : alk. paper)
 1. Cooking, India--Juvenile literature. 2. Food habits--India--Juvenile literature. 3. India--Social life and customs--Juvenile literature. I. Title.
 TX724.5.I4V425 2014
 641.5954--dc23
                        2014012905

This edition first published in 2015 by Bellwether Media, Inc.

No part of this publication may be reproduced in whole or in part without written permission of the publisher. For information regarding permission, write to Bellwether Media, Inc., Attention: Permissions Department, 5357 Penn Avenue South, Minneapolis, MN 55419.

Text copyright © 2015 by Bellwether Media, Inc. PILOT, EXPRESS, and associated logos are trademarks and/or registered trademarks of Bellwether Media, Inc. SCHOLASTIC, CHILDREN'S PRESS, and associated logos are trademarks and/or registered trademarks of Scholastic Inc.

Printed in the United States of America, North Mankato, MN.

Table of Contents

Cooking the Indian Way	4
Eating the Indian Way	6
Regional Foods	8
Chai and Sweets	10
Getting Ready to Cook	12
Raita	14
Vegetable Biryani	16
Aloo Gobi	18
Tandoori Chicken	20
Glossary	22
To Learn More	23
Index	24

Cooking the Indian Way

Indian people look to religion for daily guidance, including what foods belong on their plates. Those who follow **Hinduism** do not eat beef. This is because they believe cows are **sacred**. People of the **Muslim** faith do not eat pork. Their **holy** book, the Quran, forbids it. Many **vegetarians** are of the **Jain** religion. Their strong belief in nonviolence prevents them from eating animal meat.

Meat or no meat, Indian **cuisine** is heavily spiced. The spices are what define an Indian dish. Those used most often include cumin, coriander, and turmeric. Dishes cooked with a mixture of spices are called **curries**. A blend of spices, called *masala*, often seasons a curry to add even more flavor and heat to it.

Home of Spice
About 50 different spices are grown in India.

Eating the Indian Way

The **traditional** way of eating in India is without forks, spoons, or other utensils. Indian people view their hand as the only utensil they need. They do make sure to eat with just their right hand. The left hand is used for unclean things like wiping in the bathroom. Sometimes a piece of *naan* or *roti* bread is used to scoop food.

Namasté

Indian people sometimes use the *namasté* gesture to express that a meal was satisfying. To do this, people put their palms together in front of their hearts and bow their heads.

Meals are a time to gather many **generations** together. This means an Indian table is large and has many seats. Dishes are arranged in the center of the table to make it easy to share. Feasting together is one way Indian people celebrate all of their major holidays.

Regional Foods

Indian dishes are not prepared the same way across the whole country. Different foods are popular in each region. Indians in the north love to eat roti. Rice is a favorite of those in the south.

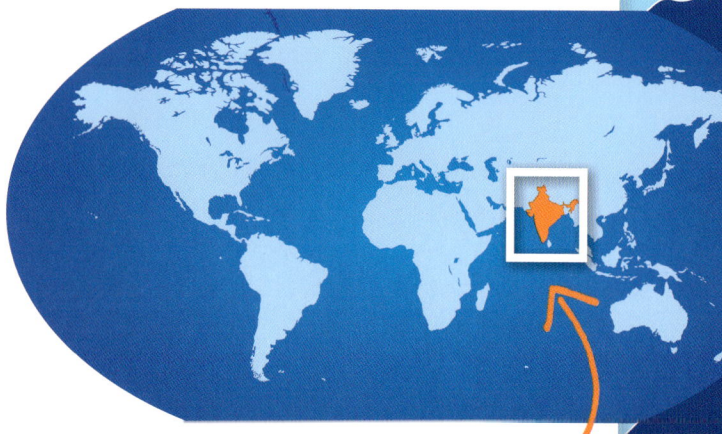

Where is India?

West Bengal
rasgulla:
Dessert dumplings made with Indian cottage cheese and cooked in a sugary syrup

Gujarat
thepla:
Spiced flatbread made with dried methi leaves

Nagaland
momos:
Steamed dumplings stuffed with ground meat

Tamil Nadu
sambar:
Vegetable stew made with lentils and a tart tamarind broth

Chai and Sweets

Indian people are regular tea drinkers. *Chai* is their word for tea. It usually refers to black tea with milk. Spices are often added to tea to create masala chai. Tea was once a drink of royals, but now it is enjoyed by everyone. Like British people, Indian people regularly take a tea break in the afternoon.

masala chai

Top Tea Producer
The Himalayan Mountains of India are a hot spot for tea plantations.

barfi

Indian sweets are enjoyed after spicy meals and for festivals such as **Diwali**. Most are milk-based and many are flavored with coconut. Sweets are cooked rather than baked. A fudge called *barfi* is very popular. It is flavored with fruits, nuts, and spices.

Getting Ready to Cook

Before you begin cooking, read these safety reminders. Make sure you also read the recipes you will follow. You will want to gather all the ingredients and cooking tools right away.

Safety Reminders

 Ask an adult for permission to start cooking. An adult should be near when you use kitchen appliances or a sharp knife.

 Wash your hands with soapy water before you start cooking. Wash your hands again if you lick your fingers or handle raw meat.

 If you have long hair, tie it back. Remove any bracelets or rings that you may have on.

 Wear an apron when you cook. It will protect food from dirt and your clothes from spills and splatters.

 Always use oven mitts when handling hot cookware. If you accidentally burn yourself, run the burned area under cold water and tell an adult.

 If a fire starts, call an adult immediately. Never throw water on a fire. Baking soda can smother small flames. A lid can put out a fire in a pot or pan. If flames are large and leaping, call 911 and leave the house.

 Clean up the kitchen when you are done cooking. Make sure all appliances are turned off.

Raita
rah-ee-TA

Did You Know? The word *raita* is a combination of two Hindi words that mean "pungent" and "black mustard."

Cucumber and Yogurt Sauce
Serves 4

Raita is a common side dish often served to offset spicy or hot foods. It can also be served as a dip, side, condiment, or salad.

What You'll Need

- 1/2 cup plain yogurt
- 1/2 cup chopped cucumber
- 2 tablespoons chopped fresh cilantro (substitute: mint)
- 2 teaspoons chopped green onions
- 1/4 teaspoon ground coriander
- 1/4 teaspoon ground cumin
- salt
- medium bowl
- spatula

Let's Make It!

1

In a medium bowl, add the yogurt, cucumber, cilantro, green onions, coriander, and cumin.

2

Stir well, then add salt to taste. Serve chilled.

Enjoy!

Perfect Pairings

Raita can be used in many dishes. Some common pairings are the following:

- with rice
- with spicy foods
- with other vegetables as a salad
- as a dip for bread, chips, or vegetables

Vegetable Biryani
beer-YAH-nee

Traditional Indian Rice Dish
Serves 4

Biryani has been served in India for hundreds of years and was once reserved for royalty. Today, it is often prepared for weddings and other celebrations.

What You'll Need

- 1 1/2 cups basmati rice
- 1 tablespoon olive oil
- 1 chopped onion
- 3 cups vegetables (carrots, green beans, cauliflower, potatoes, peas)
- 1 teaspoon tomato paste
- 1/2 teaspoon chopped green chilies
- 1 teaspoon garam masala
- 1/4 teaspoon ground turmeric
- 1/2 teaspoon toasted cumin seeds
- 1/2 teaspoon chili powder
- 4 chopped roasted cashews (optional)
- 1/2 cup plain yogurt (substitute: raita)
- chopped cilantro
- medium saucepan with lid
- large saucepan
- spatula
- oven-safe dish
- aluminum foil

Let's Make It!

1

First, let's make the rice

1. Add the rice to the saucepan, then cover with water. Stir the rice, then drain the water. Repeat until the water is clear when drained.
2. Fill the saucepan with water. Let sit for 30 minutes, then drain the water.
3. Add 2 1/2 cups of water to the rice, then bring to a boil over high heat. Cover the pot with the lid, then reduce the heat to low. Cook for 15 minutes or until the water is absorbed.

2

Preheat the oven to 250 degrees Fahrenheit. Pour the olive oil in a large saucepan over medium heat, then sauté the onion, carrots, green beans, cauliflower, and potatoes for 5 minutes.

3

Stir in the peas, tomato paste, green chilies, garam masala, and turmeric, then cook for another 4 minutes.

4

Spread half of the rice evenly at the bottom of an oven-safe dish. Add the cooked vegetables on top of the rice.

Enjoy!

Spread the rest of the rice evenly on the vegetables, then sprinkle the cumin seeds, chili powder, and cashews on top. Cover the dish with aluminum foil, then cook in the oven for 15–20 minutes. Serve with plain yogurt or raita and chopped cilantro.

Persian Connection

Biryani was first made in the area now known as Iran. Its name comes from the Persian word *Birian*, which means "to fry or roast."

Aloo Gobi
AH-loo GO-bee

Spicy Cauliflower and Potatoes
Serves 4

Aloo gobi is a popular Punjabi dish originally made in northwestern India. There are many ways to prepare aloo gobi. Each region in India uses different spices.

What You'll Need

- 2 tablespoons vegetable oil
- 1 teaspoon cumin seeds
- 2 teaspoons garam masala (substitute: curry powder)
- 2 teaspoons turmeric
- 4 sliced garlic cloves
- 2 minced medium onions
- 1 teaspoon salt
- 1/2 inch peeled, grated ginger
- 3 large diced potatoes
- 1 head chopped cauliflower
- 1/2 cup water
- fresh chopped cilantro
- sliced scallions
- medium saucepan with lid
- spatula

Let's Make It!

1

Pour the vegetable oil in a saucepan over medium-high heat, then add the cumin seeds, garam masala, and turmeric. Fry the spices for about 30 seconds.

2

Reduce the heat to medium low, then add the garlic, onions, ginger, and salt. Fry for about 10 minutes.

3

Add the potatoes, cauliflower, and water, then cover and cook for 20-30 minutes. Check occasionally to make sure there is still water in the pan, and add more if necessary.

4

Remove from heat, then allow the extra water to evaporate.

Enjoy!

Transfer to a plate, then serve with fresh cilantro and scallions.

Did You Know?

Aloo gobi is named for its two main ingredients. *Aloo* means "potato" and *gobi* translates to "cauliflower."

Tandoori Chicken
tahn-DOO-ri

Oven-baked Chicken
Serves 4

Tandoori chicken originated in northern India. First made by a small restaurant in the 1920s, this popular dish of crispy, marinated chicken has become a favorite meal around the world.

What You'll Need

- 1 cup plain yogurt
- 5 mashed garlic cloves
- 1/2 inch peeled and chopped ginger
- 1/2 cup olive oil
- 3 tablespoons tomato paste
- 3 tablespoons garam masala
- 2 tablespoons sweet paprika
- 2 tablespoons fresh chopped cilantro
- 1 tablespoon salt
- 2 tablespoons pepper
- 4 quartered chickens
- large bowl
- spatula
- knife
- 2 large resealable plastic bags
- paper towels
- roasting pan

Let's Make It!

1
In a large bowl, combine the yogurt, garlic, ginger, olive oil, and tomato paste, then stir in the garam masala, paprika, cilantro, salt, and pepper.

2
Divide the mixture into two resealable plastic bags.

3
Use a knife to make deep slits in each piece of chicken, then divide the chicken between the plastic bags. Allow the chicken to marinate in the refrigerator overnight.

4
Preheat the oven to 500 degrees Fahrenheit. Remove the chicken from the plastic bags, then use a paper towel to absorb the extra marinade.

5
Place the chicken in a roasting pan, then cook for 20 minutes. Flip the chicken pieces over, then cook for another 10 minutes or until done.

Enjoy!

Remove the chicken from the oven, then serve with rice or bread.

High Heat
Tandoori chicken was first prepared in a clay oven that is traditionally used to cook bread. The oven's high heat made the chicken crispy on the outside and tender on the inside.

Glossary

cuisine—a style of cooking unique to a certain area or group of people

curries—foods cooked with a mix of spices

Diwali—a Hindu festival of lights; Diwali is held in October or November.

generations—groups of family members that have a wide range of ages

Hinduism—the most common religion in India; Hindus believe in many gods and that people return to life in a different form after they die.

holy—of or relating to a religious purpose

Jain—a religion in India that teaches nonviolence to animals and other people

Muslim—a believer in the religion of Islam; Islam is a major religion of India.

sacred—treated with great respect by a religion

traditional—related to the stories, beliefs, or ways of life that families or groups hand down from one generation to another

vegetarians—people who do not eat meat

To Learn More

AT THE LIBRARY

Bartell, Jim. *India*. Minneapolis, Minn.: Bellwether Media, 2011.

Hankin, Rosemary. *An Indian Cookbook for Kids*. New York, N.Y.: PowerKids Press, 2014.

Rau, Dana Meachen. *Recipes from India*. Chicago, Ill.: Capstone Raintree, 2014.

ON THE WEB

Learning more about India is as easy as 1, 2, 3.

1. Go to www.factsurfer.com.

2. Enter "India" into the search box.

3. Click the "Surf" button and you will see a list of related web sites.

With factsurfer.com, finding more information is just a click away.

Index

aloo gobi, 18-19
beverages, 10
customs, 4, 6, 7, 10, 11
desserts, 11
influences, 4
ingredients, 5
location, 8
manners, 6
preparation, 12
raita, 14-15
regional foods, 8-9
safety, 13
spices, 5, 10, 18, 11
tandoori chicken, 20-21
techniques, 5, 11
vegetable *biryani*, 16-17

The images in this book are reproduced through the courtesy of: Shutterstock, front cover; Joseph Gough, front cover (large bottom), pp. 5 (right), 7 (top); highviews, title page, pp. 9 (top right), 11 (bottom); Sasha Davas, credits page; Viktor1, table of contents; threeseven, p. 4; Pikoso.kz, p. 5 (left); Hemant Mehta/ India Picture/ Corbis, p. 6; Frans Lemmens/ Getty Images, p. 7 (bottom); MBahuguna/ Canstock, p. 9 (top left); bonchan, p. 9 (bottom left); Mukesh Kumar, p. 9 (bottom right); Wiktory, p. 10 (left); hadynyah, p. 10 (right); imagedb.com, p. 11 (top); allindiaimages, p. 12 (left); Uniquely India/ Glow Images, p. 12 (right); Shyamalamuralinath, p. 13; Yulia Davidovich, p. 15 (bottom); Ashwin, p. 23; all other photos courtesy of bswing.